JUSTIN'S
pumpkin patch adventure

Tamika L. Prince

Illustrated by Devin Smith

Published by: Just'n Tyme Products LLC

ISBN: 978-1-7320444-0-1

Printed in the United States

To my dear son, Justin Prince—this book is dedicated to you. I love you and I am thankful to be your mom. Thank you for your inspiration to be the best person that I can be. You have helped me to grow and brought me so much joy along the way. To my sweet boy, Jaxon Prince—I love you too and your book dedication will be coming soon.

Bright and early Monday morning, Justin went to school and sat in the yellow chair with his name on it. Justin's teacher, Miss Rachel, said, "Today, kids, we are going to learn about pumpkins. On Friday, we will take a trip to the Pumpkin Patch, a garden where pumpkins grow. At the Pumpkin Patch you will be able to pick out your own special pumpkins."

The kids sat quietly as Miss Rachel picked up some seeds. "A farmer plants these seeds in the ground. Pumpkins need sun and water to grow nice and round.

They have bright green leaves and brown stems that grow on the outside. They also have yummy orange pulp on the inside."

Wow, thought Justin as he sat there imagining what pumpkins looked like. *What do they feel like? How big are they?* he wondered. Justin could not wait to see them up close.

The next day, Tuesday, Miss Rachel brought in a pumpkin for the kids to look at. Justin jumped up to take a closer look. "The pumpkin is big and orange," he said. The kids' faces lit up as they followed behind him to see the pumpkin, too.

TUE

Then, he tried to pick it up. "It is hard. It is heavy," he said. Miss Rachel said, "Some pumpkins are tall and lumpy, and some are small and light. At the Pumpkin Patch on Friday, you will find one that is just right."

On Wednesday, Miss Rachel brought in some tools. She said, "Today I am going to use these tools to cut into the pumpkin and give it a silly face." So they all gathered around in a circle and watched as Miss Rachel cut out small pieces little by little. "It has triangle-shaped eyes, a circle-shaped nose, and a jagged mouth. Can you show me one of your silly faces," she said?

WED

All the kids put on the silliest faces they could think of. Justin turned his head to the side, stuck out his tongue and out came a funny roaring noise. His friends giggled.

Then it was Thursday. Only one more day left until it was time to visit the Pumpkin Patch. It was just before lunch when Miss Rachel sat all the students down for a big surprise. She said, "Everyone, close your eyes. Now open." Justin opened his eyes to a bright light. Miss Rachel put a candle inside of the pumpkin and now the face was glowing. It was a magical moment for Justin and his friends.

She said, "Okay, kids, that was our final lesson on pumpkins for the week. Tomorrow we will go to the Pumpkin Patch and you will pick out your own special pumpkins."

Pumpkins were the only thing that Justin could think about Thursday night at home. He could not wait to go to the Pumpkin Patch to pick out his own special pumpkin. He said, "Mommy, can I go to the Pumpkin Patch now?" She said, "You get a good night's rest and then when you wake up in the morning, it will be time." So Justin kissed his mother goodnight and went off to sleep.

It was finally Friday. Today was the big day that Justin had been waiting for all week. He woke up and jumped out of bed. As he was getting dressed, he thought about all the things he learned at school that week with his friends. Now the day was finally here, and Justin was off to the Pumpkin Patch!

He arrived at the Pumpkin Patch full of energy. As the kids gathered around, the farmer said, "We are going to get on this big red tractor and take a ride around the farm." They all sang "Old MacDonald Had a Farm" and other songs along the ride.

After a short ride around the farm, they came to the Pumpkin Patch. "We are here!" the farmer said. The kids hopped off of the tractor and ran up to the patch. They walked up and down the patch looking for the perfect pumpkin. Justin tried picking up the first one he saw, but it was too heavy.

He walked a little further down the patch and saw another pumpkin. It was too small and lumpy. Then he stepped over the big green leaves and walked over to the next row in the patch. The first pumpkin he saw under the green leaves was white. Although they were all beautiful, none of them were what he had hoped for.

Just before he started to walk away, he looked down and saw the one he had hoped to find. It was round. It was orange. It was smooth and had a nice long brown stem. It was everything that he imagined it would be! Justin quickly pushed backed the big green leaves, picked up his special pumpkin, and ran back to the tractor.

"What a fun trip," said Miss Rachel. "Our last stop on this Pumpkin Patch field trip is for some homemade ice cream. Let's all sing the pumpkin song." Justin started it off. "Pumpkin, pumpkin small and bright." The others joined in. "From your seeds, you grew with might."

PMPKN

They sang the pumpkin song all the way back to the front of the farm. Justin could not wait to get home to share his Pumpkin Patch story with his family. He was ready to cut into the pumpkin and taste the yummy pulp. His first field trip to the Pumpkin Patch was a fun time he would never forget.

The End!

Acknowledgments

Thanks to my husband for your unwavering support of this book and all of my endeavors. Thank you to those who provided input on the book and the publishing process: Dr. Sonia C. Leverette, Pastor Sean Dogan, Satreva Dogan, mom, family and friends. I love you all dearly. Devin Smith and Sophie Thomas, thanks for helping bring my vision to life. Last but not least, special thanks to Strawberry Hill U.S.A. for the inspiration and lasting memories that were created during our farm visit!

CPSIA information can be obtained
at www.ICGtesting.com
Printed in the USA
LVHW07s2159080918
589519LV00005B/7/P